Little Bridge Farm

Smudge Finds the Trail

All Smudge the Labrador pup's friends
have a special talent – except for him!
Can Smudge find out what he's good at?

Look out for all the Little Bridge Farm books!

Oscar's New Friends

Smudge Finds the Trail

Tiger's Great Adventure

Dilly Saves the Day

Little Bridge Farm

Smudge Finds the Trail

PETER CLOVER

Illustrated by Angela Swan

■SCHOLASTIC

First published in 2007 by Scholastic Children's Books
An imprint of Scholastic Ltd
Euston House, 24 Eversholt Street
London, NW1 1DB, UK
Registered office: Westfield Road, Southam, Warwickshire, CV47 0RA
SCHOLASTIC and associated logos are trademarks and/or registered
trademarks of Scholastic Inc.

10 digit ISBN 0 439 95098 8
13 digit ISBN 978 0439 95098 5

British Library Cataloguing-in-Publication Data
A CIP catalogue record for this book is available from the British Library

Printed in the UK by CPI Bookmarque, Croydon, CR0 4TD
Papers used by Scholastic Children's Books are made from wood grown in
sustainable forests.

7 9 10 8

This is a work of fiction. Names, characters, places, incidents and dialogues are
products of the author's imagination or are used fictitiously. Any resemblance
to actual people, living or dead, events or locales is entirely coincidental.

www.scholastic.co.uk/zone

To Yvette and Bruno

Chapter One

"Hide and seek. Hide and seek. She'll never find me!" Smudge the little Labrador puppy thumped his tail excitedly, and took a peek from his hiding place beneath White Stone Bridge.

Smudge could see his friend, Oscar the pony, cantering round his field. And lots of woolly sheep grazing on the green, rolling hills behind the farmhouse.

Little Bridge Farm is such a big place! Parsley will never find me here! Smudge thought.

Dilly the duckling came sailing past, bobbing up and down on the river. Dilly wasn't the best swimmer on the farm. She had been badly scared by a fox when she was young. Normally, Dilly would never try to swim in Willow River on her own. And she never, ever swam past the safety of the bridge. She must have been feeling very brave today.

Suddenly, Dilly spotted Smudge.

"Quaarrrrcckkkkk!" Dilly fluffed out

2

her feathers in alarm and wobbled dangerously. "You gave me such a fright, Smudge. I thought you were a fox." The scruffy duckling bobbed about on the water and smoothed down her ruffled feathers. "What are you doing down here, hiding beneath the bridge?"

Smudge peeped out, then quickly ducked back beneath the bridge.

"Shhhhh!" he whispered. "I'm playing hide and seek. I've been here for ages. But, hee hee, I haven't been found yet!"

Dilly paddled her legs wildly to keep herself in the same spot.

"You're very good at paddling in one place," said Smudge. "But would you please paddle a little further away? In case Parsley sees you!"

"Parsley? You're hiding from Parsley?" quacked Dilly. "Is that why she's dashing around the farmyard? I wondered who she was looking for."

"It's me. It's me," yapped Smudge. "Parsley's looking for me!"

Dilly flapped her wings excitedly.

"You won't tell Parsley where I'm hiding, will you?" asked Smudge.

"Oh no," said Dilly. "Your secret is safe with me. I won't say a word." Then she made a clumsy turn, splashed Smudge with water, and bobbed back up Willow River towards the safety of the farmyard.

Smudge shook himself dry and tucked himself back under the bridge to wait. Suddenly, he heard a noise up on the bridge above his head. He sat up sharply.

I wonder if it's Parsley, he thought. The little puppy held his breath. But the noise didn't sound like the normal scrabble of Parsley's nails. It was more of a tip-tappy, clip-cloppy sound.

Smudge decided to creep out of his hiding place and investigate. He poked his nose out and sniffed the air. Smudge recognized the scent straight away. The smell was very strong! He crept further out and twisted round to look up.

Filbert the mountain goat was tottering nervously on the bridge. His skinny legs were trembling as he peered down, over the bridge wall, at the water below.

"Oh, m-m-my. Oh, m-m-my," stammered Filbert. "It's s-s-so high up here!"

Smudge giggled to himself. "Poor Filbert." Smudge knew that Filbert didn't like heights. Filbert was a mountain goat, and often came to the bridge to try and get used to being a little bit higher off the ground. But he wasn't very good at it.

As Filbert peered down, Smudge jumped out and yapped a loud greeting. "Hi, Filbert!"

Smudge didn't mean to give Filbert a fright. But the goat let out a startled cry and ran back over the bridge towards the safety of solid ground.

"Sorry," said Smudge. "Did I startle you?"

"Yes! W-w-what are you doing under the bridge, anyway?" asked Filbert.

"Hiding," said Smudge. "I'm playing hide and seek with Parsley. I've been here for ages but she hasn't found me yet. Can you see her from up there?"

Filbert glanced towards the farm. "Y-y-yes. I can see Parsley. She's run, run, running. But she's looking in all the

6

wrong places. She'll never find you. Never find you." Filbert cheered up and gave a little dance of delight.

The clatter of a meal bucket sounded out from Big Red Barn. Filbert stopped dancing and turned to run all the way back to the farm.

"Don't tell Parsley you saw me," Smudge called after him. But it was too late. Filbert had gone.

Chapter Two

"Found you!" yapped Parsley.

Smudge almost jumped out of his skin. He had been dozing in a ray of warm sunshine when the little Jack Russell jumped under the bridge in front of him.

"It's taken me ages to find you," said Parsley, who started chasing her tail in circles. "I wish I had your Labrador nose," she said, "then it wouldn't have taken me half as long to hunt you out!"

Smudge puffed out his chest. He was just about to tell Parsley all about bumping into Dilly and Filbert, when Trumpet, the Old English sheepdog, came bounding past.

"Come and play," barked Smudge, tripping over his paws as he tried to catch up with the older dog. "Come and play hide and seek with us."

"Sorry, Smudge," said Trumpet. "I'm on my way to the fields. I don't have time to play any games today." The big, shaggy dog stopped for a moment and shook out his woolly coat. "Farmer Rob is practising for the county sheep-herding trials." Trumpet looked proud as he told Smudge all about it.

"Every year, I help Farmer Rob take home the winner's gold cup. I don't want this year to be any different."

Smudge wished that *he* could help Farmer Rob win a cup. Smudge loved being around people and sheep herding sounded very exciting. But he wasn't quite sure what sheep herding was!

Just then, the three dogs heard a high-pitched *Whee whee wheet* sound from a whistle. It was coming from the big field at the foot of Great Oak Hill.

Trumpet's ears pricked up immediately.

"I must go!" he barked. "That's Farmer Rob's signal. He's calling me to come and start the practice." The big sheepdog bounded off towards the field.

Smudge bounced up and down with excitement. "Can we go and watch?" he asked Parsley, wagging his tail hard.

"OK," agreed Parsley. "But we have to be quiet and try to sit still."

The two dogs hurried after Trumpet to watch the practice.

Parsley and Smudge settled down in the long grass at the edge of the big field and waited. Smudge could see Ethan, Farmer Rob's son, sitting not far away. Smudge bounced over to say hello. Ethan ruffled Smudge's ears.

"Hello, boy. Have you come to watch Trumpet work?"

"Woof!" Smudge covered Ethan with wet licks. With a final lick, he dashed back to Parsley. There was so much going on!

Parsley explained that Farmer Rob's whistles were all different commands for Trumpet to follow.

"Each whistle tells Trumpet which way to go," said Parsley. "Farmer Rob can send Trumpet to move the sheep in any direction he wants."

"How clever!" whispered Smudge. He settled his chin on to his folded paws and watched, trying to stay quiet.

Trumpet stood to attention in the middle of the field with his ears pricked and alert. A flock of anxious sheep were gossiping nearby in hushed bleats. Smudge thumped his tail in anticipation as Farmer Rob raised his whistle to his lips and blew.

Wheeet-wheeeo.

Smudge jumped up.

Trumpet immediately took off and ran to the right. He circled the sheep and positioned himself behind the flock.

The sheep looked backwards.

"Baaaa!" They all turned their heads

and stared at Trumpet.

The whistle went again. *Wheee-whooo*.

Trumped moved backwards and forwards, from left to right, behind the flock.

"Baaaa!" The sheep bleated noisily as they moved forward.

"This is fantastic!" declared Smudge.

"Sshhhhh!" whispered Parsley. "You're supposed to be sitting quietly!"

"Sorry!" whispered Smudge.

Wheee-oo. Wheee-oo.

Trumpet changed direction and drove the flock to the left.

Wheet-wheet.

Trumpet moved the sheep to the right.

Wheet-wheeoo-wheet.

Trumpet ran directly behind the flock and drove the sheep into a wooden pen at the end of the field.

This was all too much for Smudge. He jumped to his feet. He'd never seen anything so exciting!

But Parsley gave a big yawn.

"I've seen it all before. I'm going back to the farm," she whispered. "I buried a big bone yesterday but I can't remember where I hid it!" Then she slowly crept away.

Straight away, Smudge bounded back over to Ethan and buried a wet nose into his hand. Smudge had always had a soft spot for Ethan. It was Ethan who had found and rescued Smudge from Willow River when he'd been abandoned there on the riverbank. Someone hadn't loved Smudge enough to keep him. But Smudge could see how much Ethan loved him right from the very first moment they'd met.

Being an orphan, poor Smudge had been all alone in the world with no mum or dad to look after him. But he was happy at Little Bridge Farm, knowing that he had Ethan and all the other animals who loved him very much.

"Baa! Baaaa!" The sheep continued to complain from the confines of their pen as Trumpet sat down, pleased with his work. Farmer Rob ruffled Trumpet's ears and gave him a dog biscuit.

"Mmmm!" Smudge's ears pricked up. "There's titbits as well. This sheep herding looks brilliant!"

Then, Smudge suddenly noticed that three sheep down at the end of the field were standing in a separate group, away from the pen.

Smudge nuzzled his belly flat against the warm earth. Then he wriggled the patch on his bum. Smudge was desperate to have a go. He wanted to be a sheep herder just like Trumpet. How hard could it be?

"Sit still," whispered Ethan.

But I can do that! I can help! Smudge immediately bounded into the field to try his luck!

Chapter Three

Smudge dashed out into the middle of the field with his tail wagging wildly. The little puppy was so excited with all the sheep smells around him that he tripped over his own paws. Smudge tumbled and rolled on to his back in front of the three sheep.

The sheep were not amused. They lowered their heads and nibbled the grass.

Smudge was very eager to try everything he had seen Trumpet do.

"Come on, now," he said. "If you wouldn't mind just walking this way, please." Smudge tried his best to sound bossy and important – just like Trumpet.

But the sheep had different ideas. They didn't budge!

Smudge ran as fast as he could in a large circle, ending up behind the small flock. Then he crept slowly forwards, copying Trumpet, moving from left to right.

"Baa! Go away," said the sheep. They refused to move one, tiny bit.

They don't seem to be taking any notice of me! Smudge thought.

Smudge didn't understand what he was doing wrong. This time, he ran directly at the flock from behind. But the sheep just stood there and yawned.

Then, Smudge ran around to the front, yapping noisily.

"What are you supposed to be doing?" asked one of the sheep.

"I'm trying to round you up," said Smudge. "Just like Trumpet does."

"Baahhh ha haaaa!! I don't think so." The sheep laughed. "Trumpet is a champion herder like his father, and his grandfather before him!"

"I'm doing everything that Trumpet does," argued Smudge. "But I don't have a father or grandfather to teach me!"

The sheep stuck their noses in the air. "We don't take orders from just anyone, you know."

Suddenly there was a shrill whistle.

Wheet-wheeeo!

Smudge watched with his mouth open as Trumpet streaked over to collect the stragglers.

Farmer Rob blew a series of further commands and Trumpet began to drive the sheep towards the pen, nipping gently at their heels.

Smudge barked and yapped loudly as he darted in and out of the big dog's legs, trying to help.

"What are we doing now?" asked Smudge.

Farmer Rob peeped his whistle.

"What does that mean?" asked Smudge.

Wheet. Wheet.

"Do we turn left? Or does that mean right?" Smudge had so many questions that poor Trumpet couldn't concentrate on what he was supposed to be doing.

One sheep broke free and ran all the way back down to the other end of the field.

Farmer Rob didn't look very pleased.

The sheep sniggered as Trumpet lifted Smudge gently by the scruff of his neck and dropped him softly back in the long grass at the edge of the field.

"I'm sorry, Smudge," said Trumpet. "But you're just getting in the way."

Smudge's tail drooped between his legs as he crept over to Ethan while Trumpet went back to doing his job.

Wheet-wheet. Whee-whooo. Farmer Rob's whistle blew again and Trumpet leapt into action. He quickly bounded down to collect the difficult sheep.

"Baa!" The three sheep gave in as Trumpet used all his years of experience and rounded them expertly into the wooden pen with the others. Then Trumpet came over to Ethan and Smudge.

The little puppy peered up at the big dog and whimpered.

"It's no good," said Trumpet. "You're a

Labrador retriever, *not* a sheepdog. You can't herd sheep. Rounding sheep is not what you are good at."

Ethan fondled Smudge's ears.

"But what *am* I good at?" asked Smudge. "If I can't herd sheep, what else can I do?"

Trumpet shook his head.

"You have to learn for yourself the thing that you are good at," he said, wisely.

Poor Smudge felt very sad as he left Ethan and wandered away from the field. Smudge sniffed at the ground and followed Parsley's scent back to the farm.

Chapter Four

On his way back to Big Red Barn, Smudge went past the edge of Albert Wood.

There were some very interesting smells wafting his way. A squirrel. A rabbit. Smudge's nostrils twitched.

What's that?

He sniffed again.

Oh, yes. A pair of grouse.

Normally, Smudge would have stopped to investigate each of these new scents.

But Smudge wasn't feeling his usual self at the moment. He kept thinking about what Trumpet had said. Smudge had to find out what he was good at. What could it be?

As he came to the end of the wood, the trees thinned out to a single row which lined the road by Willow River.

Smudge looked up and saw Old Spotty with her young nephew, Socks. The two pigs were walking slowly into Albert Wood. Everyone on the farm knew that Old Spotty had a soft spot in her heart for Socks.

Smudge cocked his head to one side.

I wonder where those two are going off to on their own.

It was just too much for the little puppy to resist. He left Parsley's trail, and followed the two pigs into the wood. Bright sunlight filtered down through the shady leaves and branches.

Smudge stood by a flowering bush and watched. Old Spotty was teaching

Socks how to root for food, hidden beneath the leaves and moss of the woodland floor.

"What I want you to do today," explained Old Spotty to her nephew, "is to practise your snouting."

Smudge sat down and thumped his tail as the practice began.

"You use your nose – or your snout," oinked Old Spotty. "That's why it's called snouting!"

Smudge pricked up his ears to listen. He wanted to snout for roots just like

Socks. *How hard can it be?* Smudge wagged his tail.

"At first," began Old Spotty, "we gently move our snouts above the earth, sniffing the soil. Not too hard. Not too softly. Then we push our snouts carefully beneath the leaves and moss."

Smudge inched his way closer.

I bet there's a big juicy bone under there!

"Now breathe deeply," urged Old Spotty.

Socks and Smudge both sucked in their cheeks.

"Close your eyes and smell the tender roots and fresh young bulbs," said the old pig. "Then simply sniff them out. Your snout will twitch and tell you exactly where to dig."

"You make it sound so easy," oinked Socks.

Smudge wriggled the patch on his bum. He could hardly wait to try snouting out for himself. But Smudge sat quietly and watched as Socks sniffed and snouted, then used his trotters to dig up a wonderful pile of delicate roots and juicy bulbs.

"Well done, Socks," said Old Spotty. "That was almost perfect."

Smudge saw Socks's cheeks blush pink with pride.

Then Old Spotty poked at the pile of delicacies with the point of her trotter. "You were a little heavy with your digging," she said. "Some of these tender roots and baby bulbs are broken in half."

Socks looked disappointed.

"If there were any delicate truffles here," explained Old Spotty. "They would have been mashed to pieces. But it was a splendid first attempt. Well done!"

Smudge couldn't sit still any longer.

I wonder what all those roots and bulbs taste like?

He couldn't wait to dig up something of his own.

"I can do that," he said, bounding forward into the clearing where the two pigs were standing.

Socks jumped up with excitement.

"Hi, Smudge. I didn't see you standing there!"

Old Spotty peered down her snout and frowned.

"I've been watching," yapped Smudge, excitedly. "Snouting practice sounds so wonderful. Sniffing out and digging for food! Do you think I could have a try?"

Old Spotty puffed out her enormous cheeks.

"Well. . ." She hesitated. "I don't know. . . After all, you're not a pig!"

Smudge sat back on his haunches and looked up at Old Spotty, pleadingly.

"I could tell him what to do," suggested Socks. "We could do it together!"

The old sow snorted a low grunt.

"I might find some really BIG roots!"

"Very well," she agreed, cautiously. "I

don't suppose it will do any harm!"

This could be the thing I'm good at, thought Smudge, hopefully.

Under Old Spotty's watchful eye, Smudge and his friend set about sniffing out more food.

Smudge sniffed and snuffled the soft earth just like Socks had told him.

"This is easy-peasy," said Smudge. His sensitive Labrador nose easily picked up the scent of tender roots and bulbs hidden beneath the soil. Smudge closed his eyes and took a deep breath.

Yes, there are definitely loads here, Smudge thought. *Maybe even a bone or two!*

But Smudge's nose wasn't like a pig's snout. As he sniffed and snuffled, some loose earth got sucked into his nostrils. It itched and itched until. . . *Aitchoo!* Smudge let out an almighty sneeze. And once he'd started sneezing, he couldn't stop. But it didn't stop Smudge from

digging. He was so excited at the thought of finding food that he couldn't stop digging, either! It seemed the more Smudge sneezed, the faster he dug.

"Wow! That's brilliant!" Socks was impressed at the enormous crater that his friend had made. Old Spotty was less impressed.

"Harrummphhh!" She shook her head quickly from side to side. Her leathery ears slapped against her pink cheeks as she looked down at the pile of delicious treats that Smudge had ... shredded!

"You didn't listen," she said. "You dug far too quickly. I knew this was a bad idea. You are a Labrador, *not* a pig. You cannot root around delicately. You are just no good at digging for roots."

Poor Smudge was crestfallen. He was really hoping to be good at snouting and digging for roots. He wasn't.

"But what am I good at?" asked Smudge.

"There must be something!" said Socks, trying to cheer up the little puppy.

But Smudge felt really miserable as he

slunk away, back towards Big Red Barn.

"Will I EVER find out what I'm good at?" he asked himself.

Chapter Five

As Smudge crossed the farmyard, he peered up into the maple tree. The roosting branches were empty. All the hens were in the chicken coop with their baby chicks. A big black rooster sat on the roof with a snooty look, overseeing his coop.

Smudge heard the sound of excited "peep peep peeps". He ducked into the hen yard to investigate.

The mother hens had lined up twelve fluffy chicks, in two rows of six.

"Now pay attention, everyone," said a matronly, brown hen. The pink comb on the top of her head wobbled as she gave her instructions.

"Today, we are going to practise the skilful art of clucking."

Maybe I would be good at clucking like a chicken? thought Smudge.

The big hen puffed up her breast. "Two neat and tidy rows, please. Wings down. Heads up!"

A second, white hen scratched at the grit in the earth as she marched up and down, between the two lines of chicks.

"Listen to everything carefully," said the white hen, bossily. "And copy everything that we do."

Smudge took his place at the end of the second row. He sat patiently. Listened carefully. And waited for his turn.

"First chick forward," ordered the white hen.

A tiny, fluffy, yellow chick hopped to the front of the class.

The white hen began a slow, strutting walk. The little chick followed. The hen bobbed her head up and down. The little chick copied. The big, white hen puffed out her breast, took a deep breath, and went . . . "Cluck, cluck, cluck!"

The little chick went, "Peep!"

"Maybe you tried a bit too hard," said the brown hen, kindly.

The big rooster glanced down.

"Next!" said the white hen.

Another chick hopped nervously to the front of the class.

"Copy the walk," said the big, brown hen. "Peck at the grit. Now take a deep breath."

"Cock-a-doodle-doo," went the chick. It was only a tiny, little doodle-doo, but all the other chicks peeped loudly with excitement, flapped their wings, and hopped up and down in their neat rows.

The rooster on the roof puffed out his chest feathers and declared, "That's my boy!"

Smudge thumped his tail on the ground.

I can do this! he said to himself. Smudge could hardly wait for his turn.

One by one, each chick stepped forward. Some peeped. Some clucked. And some were so nervous they made no sound at all!

Then it was Smudge's turn.

Smudge was almost bursting with excitement as he padded his way to the front of the class. Smudge wagged his tail so hard that he smacked the white hen across the bottom.

"Excuse me!" The white hen was very cross. She shook out her feathers and glared at Smudge.

"Oh, dear," said the big, brown hen. "Not a very good start."

"I told you he shouldn't be here,"

snapped the white hen. "He's a dog, not a chick. He'll never cluck like a chicken."

"Give him a chance," said the big, brown hen.

Smudge suddenly felt very nervous. He copied everything that the big, brown hen did. He copied the chicken walk. He bobbed his head. Then he puffed out his chest, took a deep breath, and . . . barked very loudly.

All the chicks were terrified and ran away.

Smudge tried to cluck again.

"Woof! Woof! Woof!"

The chicks hid beneath their mothers' wings, trembling with fright.

The white hen strutted forwards and scolded Smudge for scaring the babies.

"You are supposed to cluck ... not bark," she said. "But you are a dog, *not* a chicken. You cannot cluck like a chicken. You will never be any good at clucking."

Poor Smudge's ears drooped as he left the clucking practice with his tail between his legs. As he stood outside the hen house, Smudge could see the tiny chicks peeping out at him, one by one, from their hiding places.

Smudge really thought he would be good at clucking. But he wasn't.

"Who can tell me what I'm good at?" asked Smudge.

"You must find the thing that you are good at by yourself," said the big, brown hen kindly. "It's probably not very far away!"

Overhead, the sky turned grey. Fat drops of rain plopped on to Smudge's head.

All the animals ran quickly into Big Red Barn as a sudden thunderclap boomed. Even Farmer Rob made a dash for his cottage to escape a drenching.

But little Smudge barely noticed the rain as he followed his friends inside. He still had no idea what he was good at. He couldn't herd sheep like Trumpet. He couldn't snout for roots like Socks. He couldn't even cluck like a baby chick.

Just then, Parsley came bouncing by.

"It's only a bit of wet!" The little dog laughed as all the animals crowded into the barn. "Come on, Smudge. Let's go for a mad romp in the rain. You love running in the rain!"

But Smudge shook his head sadly. He didn't want to go and play.

*

When it was time for dinner, Parsley pushed her bone towards Smudge. But the little Labrador had lost his appetite and flopped his soft muzzle on to his crossed paws.

Much later, as everyone was snuggling down to sleep, Oscar arched his neck over the side of his stall. Oscar and Smudge had made friends when Oscar first arrived at the farm, and Smudge went out of his way to make the young pony feel welcome. Smudge knew what it was like to feel sad and lost in a new place.

The young pony blew in Smudge's ear. Oscar seemed to know that something was upsetting him.

"What's the matter, Smudge?" whispered Oscar, gently. "You've been looking glum all evening."

Smudge looked up at Oscar. He was one of Smudge's very best friends.

"I'm just not good at anything," whimpered Smudge. "I can't herd sheep. I can't dig for roots. And I can't cluck like a chicken."

Oscar affectionately nibbled the top of the puppy's head.

"Don't worry, Smudge. I'm sure that you're excellent at something. You just haven't found out yet what it is!"

Smudge looked hopeful. "Do you really think so?"

"Yes I do," said Oscar, smiling.

Chapter Six

The next morning, Smudge woke early to the sound of the farmyard cockerel crowing from the rooftop of the hen house.

Smudge lay curled in the straw next to Oscar's stall. He opened one, lazy eye and looked around Big Red Barn. All the other animals, except Trumpet, were still asleep. Lots of different snores filled the sleepy barn.

Trumpet shook out his thick, woolly coat, and sent a shower of straw flying into the air.

"Morning, Smudge," whispered the big sheepdog. "It's early practice for me today. I want to make sure that I win the gold cup for Farmer Rob, so I'm getting in as much herding as I can on my own."

Smudge huffed a big sigh and closed his eyes again as Trumpet padded out of Big Red Barn on his way to the fields.

Smudge had only been dozing for a few moments, when suddenly he heard loud, anxious barking. Trumpet was back and standing in the door of the barn, trying to wake them all up.

Smudge jumped to his feet quickly and pricked up his floppy ears. Oscar stirred in his stall. Filbert woke up with a start and butted his head against the wall. One by one, all the animals came wide awake, as Trumpet barked excitedly.

"It's the sheep," panted Trumpet. "They've all escaped from the field and wandered off."

45

"How d-d-did that happen?" asked
Filbert.

"I don't know!" Trumpet sounded
really worried. "When I reached the field
this morning, the gate was wide open.
And all the sheep had gone!"

"Well, they were all there before the storm," said Old Spotty. "I saw them myself, when everyone hurried out of the rain. Farmer Rob ran across the field, slammed the gate and then dashed into White Flower Cottage. And all

the sheep were there in the field."

"D-d-did you say 'slammed the gate'?" asked Filbert. "D-d-did you see the gate close?" The other animals looked confused.

"Perhaps Farmer Rob slammed the gate," suggested Oscar, "but it didn't close properly! Could it have bounced open?"

"Ex-ex-exactly," stammered Filbert.

"The sheep must have escaped through the open gate," said Cider the cat.

"Well," said Old Spotty, "however it happened, Farmer Rob won't be very happy if he wakes up and finds all his sheep gone!"

"And the sheep might be lost," piped up Parsley.

"Then there's only one thing to do," said Oscar. "We'll just have to find all the missing sheep and bring them back safely to the farm before anything happens to them. There's no time to lose!"

Trumpet stood to attention and took command. It was a big emergency at Little Bridge Farm. "They can't have wandered far," he said, hopefully. "Let's get out there and find them."

Everyone immediately rushed off in different directions to search for the missing flock.

"Come on, Smudge," called Parsley as she raced past everyone out of the barn. "Let's see how many we can find."

Smudge chased after her, but his heart wasn't in it and he didn't run as fast as he normally did.

"I don't know what use I'll be," Smudge muttered to himself. "I'm no good at anything."

He soon got left behind as Parsley disappeared into the distance. Smudge padded slowly after his friend.

As he crossed the white stone bridge he

saw Oscar and Amber the dog, already bringing back the first of the sheep.

"We found these nibbling plant shoots at the edge of Albert Wood," said Oscar. Smudge perked up a bit. He wondered if Parsley had found anything yet!

Smudge met Cider the tabby cat and Filbert next. Together, they had found three sheep grazing on the banks of Willow River.

"Crept up on them and t-t-took them by surprise." The hairy goat was butting the sheep gently along the path home, while the big farm cat walked alongside to keep them in line.

"All right! All right," grumbled the sheep. "We were just having a bit of a wander, that's all."

"I was just following all the others," said another. "It seemed like such a nice day for a walk!"

Smudge quickened his pace and met

Daisy and Duke, the giant shire horses, bringing home a boisterous lamb who kept trying to bounce away and spring back along the path.

Everyone seemed to be finding sheep.

"I wish I could find a sheep," Smudge said. But everyone was too busy to hear him. Even Old Spotty and Socks came past with a ewe each. Smudge was beginning to feel a little left out.

Smudge met Trumpet as he rounded up the last of the stragglers from the foot of Great Oak Hill. The big sheepdog blew a great sigh of relief as he met up with the little puppy on his way back to the farm.

But Trumpet wasn't entirely happy.

"There's still one sheep missing," he told Smudge. "And no matter how hard we search, no one can find her!"

Smudge suddenly had a thought. Wouldn't it be fantastic if he could be the one to find the last missing sheep?

Just then, Parsley came bursting head-over-heels through a hedge.

"Come on, Smudge. I've been waiting for you. I thought you'd got lost!"

"But there's only one sheep left," said Smudge.

"Then let's go and find it!" Parsley yapped.

Smudge hesitated for a moment as Parsley ran off, back towards the woods.

Then he took a deep breath and set off after her! Smudge's ears pricked up and his eyes opened wide. Smudge could smell the old scent of a sheep on the grass. It was the scent of a sheep that had passed by several hours ago. Suddenly Smudge was filled with enthusiasm.

"Perhaps I can help, after all!" Smudge said to himself. "Parsley! Parsley! Wait for me!" he called, as he bounded off into the woods.

Chapter Seven

"This is definitely the smell of a sheep," called Smudge as he raced after Parsley. Suddenly, Smudge felt very excited.

Dappled sunshine filtered down through the leafy canopy into the woods. Smudge could see Parsley up ahead, chasing her tail in circles around a tree. Smudge sniffed the ground, wagged his tail and called out.

"Here, Parsley! The sheep's trail is here. And I think it goes in three different directions."

Smudge sniffed each separate trail

very carefully as Parsley came racing over.

"What is it? What is it? Have you found something?" Parsley could hardly catch her breath.

"The first trail seems to lead down towards Willow River," said Smudge, calmly. "That's where Filbert and Cider found their sheep. The second trail leads straight into the woods."

"That's where the others found most of the flock," said Parsley.

"The third trail is different." Smudge took another deep sniff.

"This scent is much fainter than the other two." Smudge puffed out his little chest. "That means that only *one* sheep has passed this way!" But when he looked up, there was no one there to hear him. Parsley had already run off in the wrong direction.

"Parsley," called Smudge. "Come back! You're going the wrong way!" But Parsley had streaked off and didn't hear him.

Smudge lowered his nose to the scent and followed his trail. It led him away from the farm, towards the outskirts of the wood.

Smudge sniffed hard. The scent was getting stronger and stronger as he padded along. The missing sheep was nowhere to be seen, but he could see that someone had been nibbling patches of grass along the path. This *had* to be the right way!

"PARSLEY!" called Smudge. But there was no answer.

Better carry on, he thought. *I've come this far.* The trail entered the other side of the wood and the trees grew thicker. It was dark and musty underneath the dense, leafy branches. Thank goodness Smudge had a good nose and the strong scent to follow. It was beginning to feel a bit scary on his own.

Suddenly, Smudge stepped out into an open clearing. Prickly bushes grew there in thick clumps. The clearing was empty, but the sheep's scent here was stronger than ever!

"I'm getting close," said Smudge.

He looked around. What was that? He ran over and sniffed at some scraps of wool caught on the spiky twigs of the bushes. *That's definitely the same smell*, he thought.

Smudge poked his nose high into the air, sniffed again and leapt further into the wood. He was hot on the trail – he just knew it! "Don't worry!" he called out to the lost sheep. "I'm coming to get you." He hoped the sheep could hear him, wherever she was!

The trail led him out of the clearing, and back through the trees, heading towards Rabbit Rock. As Smudge climbed higher, the soft earth turned to stone.

Smudge kept a lookout for any signs of the missing sheep. When he reached the huge, bunny-shaped boulder at the end of the track, Smudge saw a small stream bubbling up through the flat, smooth stones.

Smudge sniffed the air again. The scent was really strong now. The little puppy put his nose to the ground and followed the trail down the sloping rock on to a very narrow ledge. And there, in terrible danger, was the missing sheep!

"Don't move!" Smudge called out, as the sheep reached for another nibble of juicy ferns. "Don't move at all!"

Smudge huffed a deep breath. His heart was banging against his little chest. How was Smudge going to rescue the sheep all on his own?

Chapter Eight

Smudge had come a long way to find the missing sheep. He had followed the trail all the way to Rabbit Rock. But now he didn't know what to do.

Maybe I should go for help? he thought. But then the sheep looked down over the edge for the first time and suddenly realized what danger she was in. The frightened ewe bleated, and Smudge knew that he couldn't leave her. Not for one second.

"Pleeeeeeease help me," bleated the

sheep. "I don't like it up here any more."

Smudge wondered what he could do.

The ewe dared to look over her shoulder at Smudge. Her legs trembled with fear.

"How am I going to get off this ledge?" she asked. "It's far too narrow for me to turn around! And I'm starting to feel quite dizzy."

"Try not to look down," said Smudge. "I'll soon have you out of here." But he didn't have a clue what he was going to do.

The ewe was surprised to learn that everyone was out looking for her.

"Oh dear," she bleated. "I didn't mean to cause any fuss. It seemed like such a nice morning to take a quiet stroll. And now I've ended up *here*!"

Smudge told the ewe not to worry.

"You've got to listen carefully," he said. "And do everything I say."

The sheep was so frightened that even her woolly coat was trembling.

"Just take it nice and easy," said Smudge. "And try to walk slowly backwards along the ledge."

"Baaaaackwards!!" said the sheep in alarm. "That's *impossible*!"

"No, it's not," said Smudge. "All you have to do is keep looking up at me. Look at my eyes and DON'T LOOK DOWN!"

"Don't look down!" said the sheep.

"Exactly!" Smudge barked. "Just copy me as I walk backwards and remember to take it nice and slow, slow, slow."

"Slow. Slow. Slow," repeated the ewe as she copied Smudge and took three careful steps backwards.

"You're doing very well," said Smudge. He walked backwards and kept constant eye contact with the sheep.

"Don't look down!!" bleated the ewe.

Behind the sheep, the rocky ledge

opened up on to a large square slab of flat rock, which made a much wider platform. And the slope back up to Rabbit Rock was easy-peasy. Smudge couldn't believe it – he was actually rescuing a sheep. All on his very own!

"Nearly there," said Smudge. "Not far to go now! I'll soon have you back with all your friends and family." Smudge sounded very confident, but his little heart was still banging nervously inside his chest.

"Nearly there," repeated the sheep as she took her last steps. Then she dared to look round again.

"You've made it!" Smudge told her, running over to lick her nose. "Well done! You've been a very brave sheep."

"Thank you," bleated the ewe, gratefully. "I don't know what would have happened if you hadn't found me!"

"I just followed the scent of your trail," said Smudge. "And it led me straight to you!"

"That must have been very difficult," said the sheep. "Following a trail all that way!"

Smudge felt really happy. He hadn't found it difficult at all!

"I just sniffed the ground and followed your scent."

"I'm glaaaaaaad you did," bleated the sheep.

Chapter Nine

The sheep let Smudge lead her all the way back to the farm.

"I don't remember coming this way at all," she said. "I'm always forgetting things. I don't think I would ever have been able to find my way back home."

Smudge felt very important. He puffed out his little chest and led the ewe away from the clearing and out of the woods.

Smudge didn't even need to sniff the ground to find his way back. His Labrador instincts told him which way to go. His own scent was still heavy in the air.

The ewe trotted along happily behind. "You must have thought that my friends were very rude, yesterday," she bleated. "When you were trying to herd them into the pen."

Smudge looked back at her. "That's OK," he said cheerfully. "I'm not very good at sheep herding."

Smudge told the ewe about his attempt at snouting with Old Spotty and Socks.

"I'm not very good at digging for roots either," he said. "I made a complete mess of it."

"Baaaa!!!" said the ewe. "That's because you are a dog, not a pig! Pigs have special snouts for snouting!"

"And I'm also rubbish at clucking like a hen," added Smudge.

"Baaah ha ha!" laughed the ewe. "You don't even *look* like a chicken!"

They finally arrived at White Stone Bridge. Trumpet was waiting there with all the other farmyard animals. Parsley came scampering forward with her tail wagging wildly.

"We were just about to organize another search party and come looking for you," she yapped. "We thought you were lost." Parsley was so happy to see her little friend that she nuzzled his nose and covered him with wet, slobbery licks.

"And you found the missing sheep," said Trumpet.

"You d-d-did it, Smudge," stammered Filbert.

"Well done, Smudge," snorted Old Spotty. The old sow pushed her way to the front of the gathered crowd to welcome Smudge home.

"Go, Smudge, go!" squealed Socks.

Everyone was delighted that Smudge had found the last, missing sheep and brought her back to the farm.

"Three cheers for Smudge," barked Trumpet, who bounded forward to take over and herd the silly ewe back into the field.

"If you don't mind," she bleated. "I'd like Smudge to lead me."

Smudge felt really proud as he padded

along in front with the sheep and everyone else walking behind in a long line.

When they reached the field, Oscar leaned over the gate and opened the catch with his teeth. Filbert gently butted the gate open. And Smudge led the procession into the field.

All the other sheep stood in a huddle and stared.

"Are we having a party?" asked one of the flock.

"Is it someone's birthday?" said another.

"Are we going for another walk?"

Smudge laughed and ran as fast as he could in a big circle around the field. He was so happy that he had found the missing sheep and led her home. He wished Ethan had been there to see him do it!

"I don't know what we would have done without you," said Trumpet.

"It's almost t-t-time," reminded Filbert.

"Farmer Rob will be up and about soon. Now he won't have to worry about the missing f-f-flock."

"Best get back to Big Red Barn," said Smudge. Suddenly he felt very tired. All the animals followed Smudge as he led the way back home.

Inside Big Red Barn, Smudge flopped down on to his straw. But he could see that Oscar looked very proud of his little friend.

"You've finally done it," said Oscar.

"Done what?" Smudge looked up at the pony from beneath heavy eyelids.

"You've finally found what you're good at," Oscar said happily.

Smudge wasn't sure what Oscar meant.

"Tracking down the sheep like that. You're a great *retriever*. That's what you're meant to do!" said Oscar.

"A *Labrador retriever!*" Smudge barked. "Being a *retriever* is what I'm good at!"

He lay his head on his folded paws. Just before he fell asleep, Smudge sighed a happy sigh. He was very tired, but very happy.

Everyone has something they're good at, he thought to himself. *Even me.*

Don't miss the next
title in the series!

PETER CLOVER

Little
Bridge
Farm

Tiger's Great Adventure

A bright shaft of morning sunlight filtered down through the skylight in the roof of Big Red Barn. Tiger the kitten leapt up on to a bale of straw and sat in the warm puddle of light. Just beneath the bale, she could see her five brothers and sisters, fast asleep in a warm, fluffy bundle.

Their mother, a tabby cat, lay curled in the straw next to the kittens' wicker basket. Tiger wriggled with happiness from the tip of her nose to the tip of her tail. They all looked so peaceful lying there.

It was very early and all the animals in the Big Red Barn were fast asleep.

Tiger looked around. Oscar the pony was dozing dreamily in his stall. Filbert the goat was snoring loudly. And Smudge the Labrador puppy was cuddled up to Parsley the Jack Russell. Tiger was the only animal who was awake. She had the whole barn to herself.

"Grrr!" Tiger growled to herself. She liked to imagine herself as a big, fierce tiger stalking her brothers and sisters. She would never hurt them, though she often liked to creep up on them when they weren't looking. But they were all asleep. She crouched low on the bale of hay, wondering what it would feel like to pounce into the middle of the cat basket and wake them all up!

Tiger gave another low, grumbling growl, pretending that she was the bravest, scariest, most dangerous kitten in the entire world. It wouldn't be *so* naughty, would it, to wake her brothers and sisters up? They'd be awake soon, anyway.

Tiger bristled her striped orange and white fur into a spiky ball. Her kitten fur stood on end like the prickles of a fierce, orange hedgehog.

"Grrr!" Tiger narrowed her eyes and prepared to pounce.

"TIGER!" whispered a stern voice. "Don't you dare!"

Tiger peeped down over the edge of the bale of hay. There was her mother, Cider. She had one sharp eye open, watching her. Tiger should have known.

How does mum do that? Tiger thought to herself. *She always knows when I'm about to be naughty.*

Tiger twitched her whiskers and made her short tail bush out like a fox-brush.

Cider gave Tiger a long, silent stare. She didn't need to say another word. Tiger knew if she carried on she'd be in big trouble.

Tiger decided not to pounce. Instead, she waved her tail slowly in the air. Then she jumped down from the bale and ran over to Cider to have her ears licked. Tiger didn't want to make Cider cross with her.

But as she cuddled up to her mum,

Tiger couldn't help one paw padding the ground in front of her and her tail still twitched. She was so full of energy. Just sitting still made her feel as though she would burst!

A large yellow butterfly fluttered in through the doors of Big Red Barn. Tiger watched it skitter through the air – up and down! up and down! – until it slowly flew towards Tiger. She didn't dare move and she didn't dare breathe as she watched to see what the butterfly would do next. Softly, it settled on Tiger's little pink nose.

Tiger had never seen such a beautiful butterfly before. She watched as the butterfly lazily opened and shut its golden yellow wings. The butterfly's feet tickled Tiger's nose.

Oh no! Tiger thought. She could feel what was starting to happen. Her nose itched and twitched. She didn't want the butterfly to go away.

"A... Ahh... Ahh ... choo!" Tiger sneezed. The butterfly shot off and fluttered away.

"Come back!" Tiger called after the butterfly. As Cider turned to lick behind the ears of one of Tiger's sisters, Tiger jumped up to follow her new friend. But it was too late. The butterfly flew through a small gap between the wooden doors. She was gone. Tiger huffed a sigh. Butterflies didn't make very good friends, she decided. She sat down and began to wash her nose with her paws. That always made her feel better.

Around her, the other animals began waking up, yawning and stretching. Out of the corner of her eye, Tiger could see Oscar in his stall. The pony's long tail swished below the gap in the stall-gate. That must mean Oscar was awake.

That tail would be such fun to play with! Tiger thought. As she watched the tail swish, she climbed to her feet. She took one step forwards, then another. . . She just had to do some more stalking! That tail looked such good fun to play with! Tiger flattened herself to the ground, lay her belly against the soft straw, and began to creep towards the pony's stall.

Tiger's ears pricked up as the barn's big wooden doors suddenly opened wider and Farmer Rob stepped inside. She froze and watched as the farmer walked over to Oscar.

"Morning, lad," the farmer said, giving Oscar a friendly pat on the rump. Tiger watched Oscar crane his head round to eat the sugar cube that Farmer Rob always brought for him.

Farmer Rob was taking the pony out for his morning run. Tiger knew she had to hurry if she wanted to get that tail. She kept her head low, her ears flat, and stalked her way quickly across the barn. The morning sunlight made Oscar's tail shimmer as Farmer Rob walked him towards the doors. Flick! Swish! Oscar's tail went back and forth. Tiger knew this was her last chance. She pounced.

"Yeeooowwwlllll."

She leapt through the air and stretched out her paws for a swipe at Oscar's tail. If she could just get one golden hair, that would be a brilliant prize for her stalking. But she was in such a rush, she didn't set off in a big enough jump. She could feel herself falling to the ground. Not yet! She was going to miss Oscar completely – and hurt herself. She fell to the floor with a thud. Oscar trotted past and out through the barn doors.

Tiger picked herself up out of the dust.

"Are y-y-you OK?" a sleepy voice asked. It was Filbert the goat, just waking up.

"Of course I am!" said Tiger, turning round. "I love playing in the sawdust." Tiger didn't want her friend to think she was bad at stalking.

"Oh. It's just that you looked like you might have hurt yourself," said Filbert, trotting over. Tiger ruffled her fur and tried not to look embarrassed. She could see that Filbert knew something was up. "Is there anything I can do. . .?" he started to ask. But Tiger gave him a look. Filbert didn't finish his question. "Do you have any food?" he asked, instead. Filbert was always hungry. This made Tiger feel better.

"Sorry, Filbert, I haven't," she said.

"Oh well," Filbert sighed. Then he went back to his stall.

Tiger shook the wood-shavings from her fur.

Then, Tiger noticed that the barn doors had been left wide open. And outside she could see the farmyard! She scurried over to the big barn doors, and peered out.

Her green eyes grew wide with excitement.

"Wow!" she gasped. "Just look at *that*!"

Look out for the rest of the series!

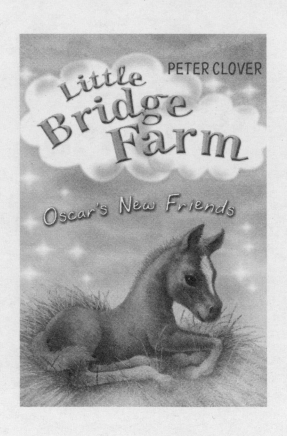

PETER CLOVER

Little
Bridge
Farm

Oscar's New Friends